MW00814311

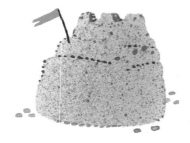

CROSSWINDS PRESS, INC.
P.O. Box 683
Mystic, Connecticut 06355
crosswindspress.com

© 2010 by Crosswinds Press, Inc.

All rights reserved. No part of this book may be reproduced
or transmitted in any form without the written consent of the
publisher except in the case of brief quotations embodied in
critical articles and reviews.

Printed in the United States of America

ISBN 978-0-9825559-4-1

10 9 8 7 6 5 4 3 2 1

Book design by Trish Sinsigalli LaPointe, LaPointe Design.
Old Mystic, Connecticut
tslapointedesign.com

This Book Was Donated by
THE NEW LONDON ROTARY CLUB

A Line in the Sand

BY CJ CONNOLLY
ILLUSTRATED BY LISA ADAMS

CROSSWINDS PRESS, INC.

To Babs…for a lifetime of "toeing" the line…….

Prologue

A Line in the Sand is the fourth book in the series that began with *Wil, Fitz and a Flea Named "T."* Mr. T is a wise old flea, a modern day Jiminy Cricket, who has decided to help Wil learn a few of life's lessons while having fun along the way.

As might be expected, Mr. T has a lot of relatives who tend to visit more often than Fitz, Wil's dog, would probably like. They all bear names made up of letters (anywhere from one to twenty-three) that provide insight into their personality and the adventure to come. In this tale, Wil finds out that not every prank is a good idea. In fact, he learns that listening to his own conscience is the best idea of all. Helping him learn this life lesson are two of Mr. T's relatives—BUGC, his trickster nephew, and his Great Uncle OHHMMMM, a Tibetan monk flea. Enjoy!

Wind, sun and surf…what a day at the beach!
For Wil and his family new memories to keep.
Fitz and Mr. T along for the ride,
Eager to romp in the incoming tide.

T's not alone this fine day in the sun,
For his nephew BUGC for a visit has come.
And Great Uncle OHHMMMM is also along,
Occasionally hitting his big metal gong!

The three fleas together make an unusual bunch,
Sitting on Fitz's head eating their lunch.
Old Uncle OHHMMMM so quiet and polite,
BUGC the opposite, looking to fight.

"Hey T!" shouted Wil into Fitz's ear,
"Want to go swimming…or play right here?
The sky is so blue and the water quite warm,
Wading and playing can do you no harm!"

"Ahem," said T as he tried to think how,
To tell Wil about his family visiting right now.
"We'd enjoy playing with you here in the sand,"
Said T with a cringe as he leapt to Wil's hand.

"What's the 'we' bit?" Wil asked Mr. T his old friend.
"Do you have some relatives here once again?
I know flea families are big…humongous,
But that doesn't mean we need them all among us."

"Well, actually I do have two kin with me,
My nephew BUGC is the one that you see,
Hanging on tightly to Fitz's right flank.
Be careful of him…he likes to play pranks!"

"While BUGC is young, Uncle OHHMMMM is not.
He's a monk of a flea from a mountain top!
As you can see he has come with his GONG...
That was the only way he'd come along."

"I'm glad to make their acquaintance," said Wil.
"Though I hope you'll want to play with me still.
I thought we could build a castle in the sand,
And for that task we can use many hands."

"Hey Wil, want an adventure?" asked BUGC the flea.
"I've got an idea…it just came to me.
We could bury your mom's water bottle under the sand,
Just take it quite carefully from her hand!"

Wil thought about the idea BUGC had,
It didn't seem too awfully bad.
It might be fun to play a trick on Mom.
"OK, BUGC, I'll play along!"

"Wil, are you sure?" asked Mr. T with concern.
As Uncle OHHMMMM around did turn.
He'd stay out of sight…he wouldn't take part.
He simply hit his gong and touched his heart.

Mr. T and his nephew jumped on to Wil's shoulder,
This seemed to make Wil even bolder.
He snuck up on Mom as she took a short nap,
And picked up her water bottle with nary a flap.

Wil dug a deep hole in the sand by Mom's side,
And into it he placed the water bottle to hide.
Just as he got done Mom woke with a start,
"Where's my water bottle? Have you seen it sweetheart?"

"Darn," thought Wil. He couldn't lie.
So he un-dug the hole, putting the sand aside.
"Here it is Mom…I was playing a prank.
I buried your water bottle, I must be quite frank."

Mom smiled at Wil and then returned to her nap.
But BUGC wasn't smiling, he had wanted a flap.
Mr. T just looked worried for he knew from the past.
That BUGC would think up another prank fast.

"Hey Wil," shouted BUGC right in to Wil's ear,
"That didn't work out, but don't have a fear.
I just had another thought, one that's quite great!
I'm sure you will like the commotion it makes!"

Then BUGC whispered his idea to Wil,
To gather up water and on Dad's back let it spill.
It seemed pretty risky, but could do no real harm.
So Wil got his bucket as T looked on with alarm.

"Ahhh…Wil are you sure you should do this to Dad?
He's taking a nap, it's the best sleep he's had.
Dad's been working long hours, he really is tired.
I'm afraid a cold splash may bring on his ire!"

Sigh

"I think it will be fun," said Wil in reply.
Uncle OHHMMMM hit his gong as T gave a sigh.
This wasn't a great thing to do…no it wasn't.
He'd rather that Wil wanted to give Dad a present.

The bucket was full, the water quite chilly.
As Wil snuck up on Dad...he was looking quite silly.
Just as he began to splash Dad on the back,
Dad jumped up real quick, he was on the attack!

"William, what's wrong? What's gotten into you son?
I know it's a prank…that you meant to have fun.
But that water was cold…and my back it was hot!
When it landed upon me I thought I'd been shot!"

"And I was sound asleep and now I am not,
So I hope you don't have another plot.
You have to be cautious and carefully deal
With how your actions make another person feel."

Wil was sorry that he had awakened poor Dad.
That was the worst idea he'd ever had.
So he turned and picked up his old bucket.
Then under his arm he did tuck it.

"Wil," said BUGC, "Sorry that prank was a bust.
But don't be disheartened, having fun is a must!
I've thought of something else we can do,
I think you will like it, it's really quite cool!"

"I don't know, BUGC," said Wil in reply.
"What is your new plan, what should we try?"
Then BUGC whispered to Wil once again,
Making T quite anxious…he was worried about his friend.

"BUGC, I don't know if this new plan is good.
It's making me feel queasy, as I'm sure it should.
If we lure little Gracie to the edge of the water,
A wave will come along and push her right over!"

This time Uncle OHHMMMM hit his GONG and then spoke,
Which startled them all, for he was a quiet old bloke.
"Wil, I have but one question for you to ponder.
If you do this to Grace, what will it do to you, I wonder?"

Wil stopped, looked down, what did he see?
A line in the sand where the ocean would be.
The waves were strong, so big that day…
They could sweep poor Gracie off and away!!!

Wil thought for a moment, then smiled and said,
"It would be really awful, it would make me feel bad.
It's not a prank or a joke like the others,
It wouldn't be nice…I'm Grace's big brother!"

Wil learned a lesson from Uncle OHHMMMM in this way.
That there are lines in the sand you can cross every day.
But once you've stepped over them you cannot go back,
You'll have lost a piece of yourself, one you'll forever lack.